Introducing Russell

Happy Reading!

Happy
Deb

Introducing Russell

*Written and Illustrated
by Debbie Walter*

Moose Run
Productions
Clinton Township, Michigan

Published by...
Moose Run Productions
P.O. Box 46281 • Mount Clemens, Michigan 48046-6281
moose-run.com

Manufactured in the United States of America

ISBN-13: 978-0-9766315-2-1
ISBN-10: 0-9766315-2-0

Library of Congress Control Number: 2007921889

Cover illustration by Debbie Walter
Printed in Michigan

This book is dedicated to…

My sister
Without whose nudging it wouldn't have gotten done!

We would also like to thank all our editors…
Ann, Colleen, Julie K., Julie M., Ksenia, and Mary
and all our prereaders…
Elizabeth, Kayla, Keegan, Matthew, Rebecca, Sarah, Taylor, and Trevor.

Your comments were appreciated more than you will ever know.

Table of Contents

Preface
A Trip Is Planned. 1

Day One
Off We Go 4
We're Here. 6
Enjoying the Rest of the Day. 9

Day Two
A New Day 14

Day Three
A Discovery Is Made 17
Off to the Vet 21
Back at the Campsite. 25

Day Four
A Bright New Day. .28
Going Shopping. 31
Meeting Alan's Family. 35
A Summer Storm 39

Day Five
Russell Moves In 41
Meeting Someone New. 44
A Busy Day 48
Another New Friend 51
The Ice Cream Place 55

Day Six
Buddy the Squirrel Returns 57
Enjoying the Day Together 60

Day Seven
Packing Up 64

Epilogue
The Holiday Letter .66

A Trip Is Planned

Once upon a time, there was a dog, a cat, and a mouse who were friends. They lived with a human who provided them with a home, food, and medical care—all for free! The dog, Jake, was adopted from a shelter. The cat, Belle, was a stray who showed up one day with her three kittens (who now have homes of their own). The mouse, Russell, was a secret friend of Belle and Jake's. The human didn't realize that Russell was a member of the household.

One day, Jake sighed as he came in after his walk and lay on the floor under a window. He had been out trying to train his human and returned from the day's lesson to tell Belle of the difficulty he was having in getting their human to understand that each and every tree must be checked for pee-mail.

"All the human wanted to do was keep moving," Jake said to Belle. "I got to pick up only two trees' worth of messages. If she keeps this up, I don't know how I'm going to deal with her on our camping trip."

Belle, looking down from her sunny windowsill, replied, "Now, if you were a cat walking on the leash, the human would be so proud of you that you'd get to go anywhere you wanted."

"Well, just remember that when we're camping, neither of us will be without a leash," Jake grumbled.

"Yes, but we'll have all those new smells," Belle said as she closed her eyes.

Poking his head out from under the couch, Russell shouted, "I'm so happy! It's my first camping trip!"

Belle opened her eyes and looked at Jake. They'd been working on a plan to pack the mouse for the trip. It was a good thing that Russell was an actor—their human never knew that all the different mice Belle had brought her since Christmas were really the same mouse!

"Have you been practicing your stuffed toy-mouse imitation?" Jake asked Russell.

Jake and Belle had planned, at first, to pack the mouse with their food, but they changed their minds when Russell said that would be delicious and just like heaven. The plan, now, was to put the mouse in with their beds and toys. The human wouldn't find the little stowaway there.

"I practice every day—watch!" cried Russell, and he crouched down, tucked his feet up, and rolled over slightly.

"Not bad," said Jake. "But, if the human looks closely at you, she'll see you're not a stuffed mouse."

"Then she'll feed me, and I will be stuffed!"

"No, silly, he means that your nose keeps moving," chuckled Belle as she gazed at her little friend. "The human packs everything for us in separate boxes, so we'll just put you in one of our boxes tomorrow before she loads them into the truck."

Off We Go

The next morning, their plan went smoothly. Belle gently dropped Russell into the box with their beds and toys. Then the human took all the boxes and put them—and the mouse—into the truck along with all the camping gear. Lastly, their human put Belle in a cat carrier and snapped the passenger seat belt through the carrier's handle. Jake jumped into the cab and sat on the bench seat behind Belle. He knew he was going on a trip and allowed his travel harness to be properly buckled.

"How does he know he's not going to the vet this time?" their human muttered. "Every time we go to the vet, he turns into a limp rag, and I have to carry the beast—who suddenly weighs a ton."

After the truck started down the road, Jake put his nose out the back window, and the smells of the familiar neighborhood changed to new and exciting ones. Even Belle, he noticed, was sniffing with anticipation. Suddenly, Jake got a whiff of something that made him feel cold and afraid. He pulled his head inside and sneezed, then began to whine nervously.

"What smell did you catch?" asked Belle, noticing how uneasy her friend had become.

"Hey, Jake, look," their human announced. "There's the shelter where I found you! Do you remember it?"

"Yeah, I do. Some smells you never want to smell again," Belle heard him reply and knew their human only heard what she called barking.

They were on their way to Bay City State Park. Their human called it one of her happiest places, and they looked forward to the trip each year. Sometimes, the weather was hot, and at other times, it felt cold, and no one went into the water. But the worst time was when it rained the whole week they were there. Belle had thought she would never get dry. This year, the sun was shining, and the day was perfect for traveling. They would get to the park, set up camp, go for a walk, and when everyone was settled in, eat—which was the nicest thing to do after walking.

We're Here

Finally, after a two-hour ride, they arrived at the state park.

"I'm glad I practiced setting this tent up at home," their human said. "Otherwise, those campers across the way would be laughing their heads off."

Jake couldn't understand why his human didn't want him to help put the tent up—he was so good at it.

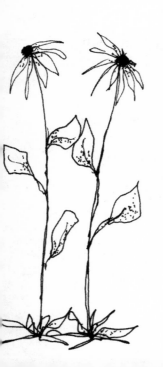

"Remember," he barked, "you have to put the stakes in first, then lift up the top."

Belle was nosing around in the unpacked boxes, looking for Russell. When she found him, he looked a bit distressed. She gently picked up the mouse, walked to the end of her tether, and placed him in the leaves. She then heard Russell happily scurrying around and remembered why she named him 'Russell.'

"Hey, Russell, want to play 'Where It's Been'?"

Russell's head popped up a foot away from her.

"Yeah, that's my favorite game!"

Belle pounced on Russell and picked him up. The mouse squeaked and yelled in his little mousey voice as the cat strutted proudly toward her human.

"Belle!" their human exclaimed. "Put that thing down. You don't know where it's been!"

Belle started laughing. "I know exactly where he's been!"

Russell jumped from her mouth and ran laughing all the way back to the leaves.

"Belle," Jake said, joining in the laughter, "you sure have trained our human to play that game."

Belle walked over to the leaves where Russell was hiding and saw his tiny nose poking out.

"Can we do it again?" Russell asked. "I can pretend to be a different mouse—I can make my voice deeper or maybe play 'almost dead' or maybe smudge dirt on my face."

"No, not right now," Belle answered. "We'll have a campfire soon, and then we'll have to go in for the night."

"But I really like it out here!" cried Russell.

"Of course you do. It's nice and warm and dry. But how much will you like it when it's cold? Or raining? Or when the mosquitoes bite your ears?"

"Yeah, they can be really tough on ears—buzzing in them too," said a new voice from the ground.

"Russell," Belle said, "I think we're about to meet someone who knows all about living in the park."

"I've seen snow and rain, sun and heat, and dogs who dig and squirrels who steal what you've worked hard to put away," came the voice again, and then from an unseen hole by the base of a tree appeared a chipmunk. "And you would think that squirrels, of all animals, would understand about saving food for winter. Hi, my name is Alan."

"My name is Belle, and this now speechless mouse is Russell. And directing the efforts of our human is Jake."

"Jake doesn't dig, does he?" Alan the chipmunk asked, eyeing the dog.

"No, he's been training our human to take him everywhere she goes. It takes a lot of his time."

"I wish him luck. I see you guys are really 'roughing it,'" chuckled Alan. "Air beds, camp stove, heater, fan. She sure is filling up that tent."

"It's my first camping trip," whispered Russell.

"Good for you!" replied Alan. "I must say, I haven't seen many humans bring mice on their camping trips—taking them home, though, is another story."

"Belle and Jake are my friends and share their human with me," said Russell in a slightly louder voice. "I'm an actor."

"At such a young age too! Come and meet my family. We'll have something to eat, and you can tell us about your career," Alan replied as he turned, flicked his tail, and disappeared down the hole.

"Go on, Russell," Belle urged. "You've got a new audience."

Enjoying the Rest of the Day

Belle strolled over to Jake and told him about the chipmunk and Russell's new adventure. Jake then told her that they were going for a walk—maybe all the way over to the boardwalk.

"Perfect," said Belle. "I'll get a few stretches in before we leave."

"Jake," their human called, "let me put on your leash first, then I can put Belle into the new kitty pack. It will be better than the newborn-baby carrier we used to use—no holes in the bottom! Now, let's go see what's changed in the park this year."

This was the best part of camping in Bay City State Park. They all enjoyed walking among the tall, old trees and watching the changing sun-and-shadow patterns that the leaves made while moving in the breeze. Jake liked the park because he didn't have to be on a short leash as he did at home. He could inspect as many trees as he wanted to while on his 16-foot retractable leash. Belle enjoyed being in the pack, watching everything from a higher point of view. Once they walked around the campground, they headed across the highway that divided the day-use area from the campground.

Some of the pathways in the picnic area had been paved, but the boardwalk to the beach made the usual 'clomp clomp' sound as they walked on it. Their noisy footsteps brought back the memories of many happy past vacations. They stopped near one of the built-in benches and looked out over the shore to the water. Jake and Belle were not allowed on the beach, but they could hear and smell the water not far away.

"The beach changes every year," marveled Jake. "I smell a few things that would be great to roll in!"

"Right. And then you'd get a bath in front of all the other dogs in the park," Belle chided. "Remember how much you disliked the last one? And only Russell and I were watching."

"It was your running commentary that made it miserable, not the soap and water."

"All right, you two. We'll go eat. You can stop all the noise," said their human as she turned back toward the campground. "But, eventually, we'll be taking all the different trails this year, so get your couch-comfortable minds and behinds ready."

After returning to their campsite, the human started to build the evening's fire in the fire pit. The wood and kindling she bought was dry and started to burn quickly. Their human set out two water dishes and a bowl of mixed dry and canned food for Jake. Belle was happy to see she'd be getting the expensive little cans of food she loved. At home, a big can was cheaper since the leftovers could be put in the fridge. But, while they were camping, she got those wonderful little cans because their human didn't want that 'fishy stuff smelling up the cooler.' Looking at Jake eating his food, Belle hoped Russell was having a good meal with the chipmunks since Jake was not about to leave one nibble behind, and neither would she.

Their human planned to cook hot dogs over the fire, and they knew they could beg a few pieces. Yes, camping was the best—their human even slept on the ground with them!

Sitting around the fire while evening fell, all three started to doze—that is until Russell showed up! He came escorted by Alan the chipmunk and his whole family, and it sounded as if each one of them was determined to win a race. The human, startled by the noise, woke up. When she saw the striped heads of the chipmunks, she went and got a bag of shelled peanuts from the truck and tossed them one by one to the noisy group. The chipmunks filled their cheeks with the loot, mumbled a quick good-bye to Russell, and ran back into the leaves.

Russell sneaked over to the wood stacked near

the fire pit. "Belle, did I miss anything good?" he asked.

"Only the s'mores," answered Belle. "But it seems you had an interesting visit with Alan and his family."

"I'm really glad I'm a mouse," Russell said. "Those chipmunks are pretty jumpy. And, having a meal with everyone talking at once—mostly complaining about squirrels and their lack of common courtesy—really makes me glad to be back here."

"So did you get a chance to show the chipmunks your acting abilities?" asked Jake.

"Well, I tried. I showed them my 'Stuffed Mousie' routine and 'Mousie in the Kitty Teeth,' but all they wanted to do was criticize! 'You don't look stuffed,' they said. 'Eat more! Can you pretend to be the kitty too? Can you roll over?' Honestly, they never stopped talking long enough to appreciate the finer points I was trying to get across!"

"Seems our little actor has a bruised ego," Belle whispered to Jake. Then, to Russell, she said, "You're going to have a challenge tonight, Russell. You're going to have to be invisible. Remember that humans, even this one, don't like sleeping with mice. We'll have our chance to get you into the tent when she takes Jake for his last walk before bed."

"Well, I hope it's soon. Chipmunks can really wear you out."

"I'll drop a few hints to our human," said Jake. "The way she keeps dozing off, she'll be as glad to get to bed as you are. Watch me whine and nudge her under the elbow."

"Are you ready for your before-bed walk, Jake?" asked his human. She hooked on his leash, and off they went. "Jake, I wish you could see all the stars tonight. Look how bright the Big Dipper is. Sure doesn't look like this at home! Oh!"

"If it weren't for me, you'd have crashed into that kid on a bike," Jake grumbled to his human, even though he knew she didn't understand. "Stars are very nice, but if you don't watch where you're going, you'll be kissing a tree next."

"Guess we'd better get back and make sure the fire is out, then go to bed," the human said.

Finally, everyone snuggled down for the night—Jake on his blanket next to his human's sleeping bag, Belle on the pillow next to her human's head, and Russell tucked in tight within the folds of Jake's blanket. All in the tent were soon asleep—except for three mosquitoes that wouldn't settle down.

A New Day

"What an awful night!" exclaimed their human the next morning. "It seemed as if there were dozens of mosquitoes in that tent. And you, little kitty, took advantage of the situation, snuggling deep into the sleeping bag and leaving me to be their late-night snack!"

Belle meowed. "Naps would be advisable this afternoon," she suggested.

The human, hearing Belle meow, said, "You're right, Belle. We need pancakes for breakfast. And we'll go for a hike afterward."

"I think you need to work on your cat 'translation' abilities," laughed Belle. "And be sure to put lots of butter on my pancakes."

Russell, who was at the door of the tent peeking out from underneath the flap, scurried over to Belle and said, "One of those mosquitoes bit my paw when I was trying to protect my ears. I can't stop scratching it, and it feels kind of funny now."

Belle looked at her little friend's paw and gave it a couple of licks. "Looks all right to me," she said. "But we'll keep an eye on it."

Jake came over to them after helping their human get all the stuff out of the truck and tent to make breakfast. "Russell, are you going to stay with your chipmunk friends all day?" he asked.

"Yes, I am."

"Well, tell them that our human will toss a few pancake pieces into the bushes and everyone can have a treat."

"I'll go tell Alan and the others right now!" Russell replied and ran off, forgetting that his paw even hurt.

After breakfast and the tossing of the pancake bits, the human once again tucked Belle into her kitty pack and put Jake on his leash, then the three began their stroll around the park. They all enjoyed the morning walks, with the smells in the air of fresh coffee and bacon frying. The breeze made the leathery oak leaves rustle, the birds were singing, and it seemed as if chipmunks were everywhere. Jake greeted a few dogs as they passed by and left a couple of pee-mail messages for others on the trees and bushes.

A child's voice called to his mother, "Look, Mom, that lady has a cat!"

"Don't be silly," the mother replied, not looking up from her morning newspaper. "No one brings a cat camping."

Their human, smiling, looked down at Belle, who definitely was a camping cat. "Belle, are you sticking your tongue out at that woman?" she asked, laughing when she saw the tip of Belle's pink tongue.

"Of course," said Belle. "Did you think I was licking butter off my whiskers and forgot to put it back into my mouth?"

"You sure are a meow-y girl this morning. Let's start our adventures by going over to the nature area to see if the great blue heron is hunting in the marsh. Then we can hike some different trails and have a picnic lunch."

It had been a beautiful summer day, and with all the walking, eating, and napping done, it only needed the evening's campfire to be the perfect vacation day. As they were sitting around the crackling fire, Russell returned from his visit with the chipmunks. He followed Belle's long tether and found her play-hunting at the edge of the brush.

"We had fun today," Russell told Belle. "And the chipmunks hope there will be pancakes for breakfast tomorrow. But I really feel tired, and my paw hurts even more. I think I'll sneak into the tent early."

Belle licked his paw and noticed it was hot and red from his scratching. "Go ahead and snuggle into the box with the dog blanket. It will be warm tonight and Jake won't need it. Maybe you'll feel better after a good night's sleep."

"If the mosquitoes will let me."

"Don't worry. Before she goes to bed, I'm sure our human will make certain there are no mosquitoes in the tent tonight."

Belle then joined their human and Jake by the fire. She jumped into their human's lap and told Jake where Russell was sleeping.

"It's pretty early for that mouse to turn in," he said. Then, with a contented sigh, he laid his head on his front paws to watch the fire.

A Discovery Is Made

The next morning, when their human was at the restroom, Russell limped over to Belle. "Belle, my paw really hurts, and I don't feel so good," he whispered.

Belle took one look at the swollen little paw and called Jake over. "I think someone will have to look at this," she said.

"I think you're right, Belle. But how are we going to get our human to understand? She's pretty smart, but after all the 'Where It's Been' games, will she even try?"

"It will take some luck, but I think we can do it."

"We don't need luck," Jake replied confidently. "We have faith."

When their human returned, she found Belle sitting outside the tent with a little mouse in her mouth. "Belle, not another one! Put it down. You don't know where it's been!"

"I know exactly where it's been and where it should be going," said Belle as she set Russell down by her front feet.

Russell just lay there quietly while the human came over to look at him.

"He's still alive. Let me have him, and I'll take him over to the bushes and let him go," their human said as she reached for Russell's tail.

"No!" cried Belle as she stopped her human's hand with a lightning-quick front paw—claws extended.

Jake trotted over and nudged Russell with his nose, exposing the swollen little paw.

"Belle, he's hurt. Let him go free, or get rid of him," the human said.

"No. He needs to have someone help him," said Belle. She gently picked Russell up and walked into the tent, then into the pet carrier.

"Belle! Get out of the tent with that mouse!" scolded their human.

Jake stretched to the end of his tether, put his paws up on the truck, and started barking.

"Jake, enough! Is this whole place going crazy? This is supposed to be a vacation!"

Hurrying into the tent, the human tried to get Belle and the mouse out of the carrier. Belle turned so she was facing the back of the crate, protecting Russell, while her behind blocked the door. Their human pulled the carrier out of the tent and tried, as carefully as possible, to shake Belle from the container through the open door. But Belle was ready for that. She had practiced the 'I Will NOT Come Out' routine each time she went to the vet.

Jake had quieted his barking to a pitiful whining and was still standing with his front paws on the truck.

"What is it with you guys today? You'd think that mouse was something special!"

"He is," growled Belle.

"Having a problem?" asked an older couple as they passed by the campsite.

"My cat found an injured mouse and took it into her carrier, the dog is whining for a ride, and I wish I could understand cat mutterings," replied the flustered human.

"Well, maybe you should take them all to an animal hospital. Maybe they could figure out what's going on," the woman offered.

"I don't know any vets around here, especially ones that will take care of a mouse."

"We do! We're the hosts here at Bay City State Park," said the man. "Our grandson has a pet rat, and although I never thought I'd say it, Kevin's rat is rather nice. He brings him to see us sometimes. I can give you the name of his vet."

"Thank you," barked Jake, and he sat down wagging his tail and extended his paw for a shake.

"Thank you," echoed the human.

"The vet's name is Benjamin Rhoads," the man continued. "And he works at the Rhoads Animal Clinic. Call the park rangers—they have the phone numbers of businesses in the area on file in their office."

"Thank you again," the human responded. "I sure am glad I charged my cell phone yesterday!"

"Come by later to the host site, and let us know how things go. I'm Ray, and this is my wife, Cheryl," he said and gave the number for the rangers' station to the human.

"I'll definitely come by."

The human made the calls and explained her problem to the man who answered the phone at the animal clinic. After he had a good laugh, he told her to bring *all* of her animals right in.

Off to the Vet

"All right, everyone into the truck. We're going for a ride."

Belle turned around once the door to the carrier was locked and tucked Russell between her paws. Jake didn't need any encouragement to get into the truck—he knew this vet visit didn't mean a shot for him. The human followed the directions she had received from the man at the animal clinic, which she was surprised she remembered, given her state of mind during the phone call. Finally, they arrived at the vet's office—a former house, which now sat between two sets of stores.

Rushing into the office with Jake on his leash and Belle and the mouse in the carrier, the human announced, "I brought everyone, just like you said. I hope you can speak 'dog' and 'cat' and 'mouse' because I need to know what's going on!"

"Come into the exam room, and we'll see the cat and mouse first," said Doctor Rhoads.

Their human set Belle's carrier on the examination table and opened the door. Belle came out with Russell in her mouth and tenderly set him down. Russell, seeing all the lights and a stranger, got scared and scurried under Belle's long fur. Doctor Rhoads carefully lifted Belle up and looked at Russell.

"His front paw has an infected bite," he said. "I can give you some antibiotic drops for your mouse that should help. You'll have to give them to him twice a day, but it should be easy—they taste sweet."

"You know," the human returned, "he's not really my mouse—I don't need a mouse who will get into the walls and chew on all my electrical wires! I was hoping you'd keep him."

"I don't think that your cat will let me keep the mouse," the doctor replied, "especially one that goes to her for comfort and protection."

"I don't understand it," the human muttered. "Why, after catching all those other mice this past year, would she pick this one to help? I don't see anything different about him. He's just another deer mouse. I was hoping you'd have some answers."

Jake barked once, stood up on his hind legs, and put his front paws on the examination table. Then both humans watched in amazement as Russell edged over to the end of the table and touched noses with Jake.

"All I know, from my years in practice, is that you never know what you'll see next," Doctor Rhoads put in. "I can't explain why animals do things like this. Just accept it as a special gift."

"A gift? My cat and dog have a pet mouse? My cat...and my dog... have a pet MOUSE!"

"Yes, we do, and his name is Russell," said Jake. He was feeling left out—Belle and Russell were getting all the attention.

"Now, now, we weren't neglecting you," said Doctor Rhoads. "We just have to get the serious stuff done first. Would you like a dog treat? The vitamins in these are good for keeping the fleas off, and all the dogs I know like them."

Doctor Rhoads scratched Jake's ears like someone who knew dogs, and Jake liked him—even if he was a vet who gave shots.

"I'll show you how to use the dropper to give the mouse his medicine," the vet continued. "And you will need to keep it refrigerated."

"We're camping and only have a cooler. Can I keep it on the ice? Will that be good enough?"

"It should. Just don't let your ice supply get low."

Russell took the antibiotic from the dropper, then turned to the human and said, "I'm a good mouse. I don't chew on the wires in your walls or run around when you have guests or steal your food. And I'm a clean mouse. Belle and Jake helped me when my family died from the winter's cold. They are my friends, and you are their human. I'd like you to be *my* human too."

"That was a beautiful speech, Russell," Jake said. "What play did you get it from?"

"It wasn't from any play—it was from my heart," Russell replied.

The passionate squeaking from the little mouse made both humans laugh in surprise. "Well, Doctor, can you translate that?"

"I'm not sure of all the words, but I think the heart of it is that not only do your cat and dog have a pet mouse—you do too! You'll have to give him a name for my records," said Doctor Rhoads.

"Just put him down as 'Belle and Jake's mouse' for now. If he is such a special gift, he'll need a special name. I'll write and tell you what it is when I find it."

Belle gently picked Russell up and strolled back into the carrier. She knew their human would take care of the mouse until he was well. Russell would be a part of their family—eventually. Belle and Jake now had the opportunity to show their human how special this little mouse really was. After paying Doctor Rhoads for his services, their human drove them back to the state park.

8

Back at the Campsite

The human put the carrier down on the ground and opened the door so she could hook Belle's tether to her collar.

"OK, mouse, now's your chance to run," the human said.

But Russell just followed Belle to a shady spot by a tree, snuggled between her front paws, and went to sleep. Going to the vet was a tiring experience.

The rest of the afternoon was a lazy one for the animals. But their human spent much of the time muttering to herself about 'gifts' and 'a mouse's mother' as she straightened up the tent and prepared the fire pit for the evening's fire.

After Jake's late-afternoon walk, the human fed him and Belle, then offered the little mouse a piece of dog food, a few pieces of cat food, and a slice of apple on a paper plate. As Russell crawled onto the plate and ate alongside the cat and dog, the human sighed.

"It seems you are not an ordinary mouse," she said. "You will definitely need the right name. How about Morris?"

Belle chuckled. "That is the name of a famous cat."

Jake laughed. "Maybe her next choice will be Lassie."

Watching the mouse eat, their human tried different names. "Stuart is a famous mouse, and he's a special mouse too. Do you like the name Stuart? How about Mickey?"

Russell moved around until his back was toward the human.

"I guess that means 'no,'" she said. "How about Squeak, like Garfield's mouse, or Koko—she's a famous gorilla. She can do sign language."

Still, Russell did not turn around.

"Those are some good choices," Jake said. "But those names belong to other animals—Russell has his own. You knew what to call me, even though the shelter called me 'Oscar,' and you knew Belle's name the moment you saw her. Keep trying. You'll get Russell's name right."

"Thanks for all your suggestions, Jake," their human laughed as the dog licked her cheek. "I just wish I spoke better 'dog' and knew what you were saying. You and Belle seem to really like this unusual mouse, so it's important to have just the right name."

"Well, at least we all agree on that," said Belle.

Later that evening, as they sat by the fire, their human continued thinking of names and trying them out on Russell. "Skyler? Ginger? Pepper? Max? Max is a good name. Do you like that one?"

Russell looked at her for a moment and moved his head side to side.

"I think you just said 'no'!" the human said in surprise. "I don't think you are just an ordinary mouse."

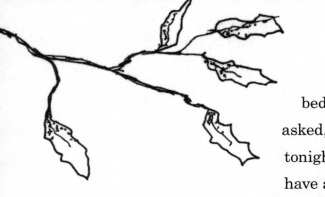

When it came time to go to bed, the human turned to Belle and asked, "Where will the mouse be sleeping tonight? I really don't think I'm ready to have a mouse share my sleeping bag."

Belle thought that was pretty funny because the human had been sharing a home with Russell for months, and it hadn't bothered her at all.

"Russell will sleep with me, next to you, on a corner of the mat that's under your sleeping bag," Belle replied. And she and Russell did just that.

"I've got to find Doctor Dolittle—I think my animals are talking!" said the human.

She then checked the tent for mosquitoes and snuggled down into her sleeping bag. After turning around three times, Jake lay down on his bed on the other side of his human.

"At least everyone knows dogs can count up to three," Belle sleepily teased Jake.

"Just something a dog has to do," said Jake with dignity. "And we can count higher than three. Sometimes we can count up to four, like you cats," he teased in return.

Their human petted the dog and cat, gently touched Russell's head, said good night to all, and turned off the light.

9

A Bright New Day

The next morning, their human awoke and counted her pets. "One dog. One cat. One mouse who needs medicine. Yep, everyone's still here."

She took out the bottle of antibiotics from the cooler, picked up the little mouse, and set him on the top of the closed cooler. She then put the dropper in front of his tiny nose, and Russell drank the drops from the end.

"We've got to find a place for you to live and somewhere you can eat, drink, and sleep safely. I know Belle and Jake won't hurt you, and you seem to live by different rules than any mouse I've ever known, so I don't want to confine you to a cage or fish tank when you enjoy their company so much. It's something I'll have to think about on our hikes. I do my best thinking then."

Their human took Jake for his morning walk, then all enjoyed a filling breakfast of bacon and eggs.

"We'll have to stop by the host site today," the human said, "to let

28

Ray and Cheryl know how the little mouse is doing and to thank them again for their kindness. Jake can go on his leash, and Belle, in the kitty pack, but I don't think putting the mouse in my pocket would be very comfortable for either of us."

Belle, after watching their human clip the leash to Jake's collar, solved the problem by picking up Russell and jumping into the kitty pack. She tucked the mouse down by her feet next to the mesh side of the pack.

"I guess that will work, Belle," said their human as she strapped the kitty pack on herself. "But you will have to be careful not to step on him or sit on him!"

On their first loop around the park, they didn't see the hosts at their site, but the second time, they found the couple sitting at the picnic table getting ready for one of the kids' craft projects they organized.

"Hi! Remember me?" the human called. "I'm the one with the mouse problem. I wanted to tell you that the vet you recommended took good care of him. Thank you so much for your help."

"We were glad we could help," replied Ray. "I know that as hosts we are expected to answer a lot of questions, but your sick mouse was a new one for us."

"I'm keeping a journal of the interesting people we meet and situations that come up, and your problem has been the highlight of the week," said Cheryl. "Where are you keeping the little mouse, and what have you named him?"

"Last night, he slept with Belle, my cat, but I want to find something he can use as a house, where he'll have food and water whenever he needs them and a safe place to sleep. I don't have a name for him yet. Nothing I tried 'fits,' and I'm beginning to feel like the queen trying to figure out Rumpelstiltskin's name."

"I'm sure you'll figure out his name. We'll stop by later and peek in on him," Cheryl returned.

"Actually, he's right here," the human said. "Belle brought him with her in the kitty pack. Look through the mesh on the side, and you can see his fuzzy face by her feet."

The hosts looked through the side of the pack, and sure enough, there was the little mouse.

"I see he's a deer mouse. They have some of the prettiest coloring," said Ray.

"And, when he looks at me with those big, innocent eyes, I just can't leave him to fend for himself," sighed the human, "though I will have to for a while. We need some groceries and ice."

"Do you need us to keep an eye on your pets?" asked Cheryl.

"No, I'll be taking them with me. I don't like to leave the animals in the truck, but I have some window gate-vents that let me keep the windows half open. That way, I won't have to worry about the truck getting too hot. Grocery shopping is the only real problem when camping with my animals. Well, that and taking a shower."

"Ah, a responsible pet owner!" exclaimed Ray. "It's always nice to see people caring for the furry members of their families."

"I agree. Thank you, again, for your help. Tell your grandson you're both heroes to a little mouse."

Going Shopping

Upon returning to the campsite, the human carefully made out a shopping list so she could get all the things she needed without wandering aimlessly. She never worried about the pet store—they welcomed animals, but she wasn't going to announce that she was bringing in a mouse as well as her cat and dog.

When she arrived at the grocery store, the human checked the parking lot and was glad to see only four cars and a parking space in the shade. With the window gate-vents in place and a stern warning to her pets to 'be good,' she was in and out of the store in 15 minutes.

"You were so good," their human offered. "We'll take a drive around town before we go to the pet store and get some food for the mouse. But, first, we've got to get the ice and food into the cooler."

That done, they took off again. They drove along some of the residential streets as their human looked at the gardens and commented on the flowers. Jake was sniffing out the window and sent 'woof' greetings to the dogs in other cars. Belle spent her time between complaining about being cooped up in the carrier and comforting Russell.

"Russell," the cat said, "the pet store is like nothing you could imagine. A huge building filled with things for people to buy for their animal companions. Our human likes to look at things for each of us, and sometimes, we give her hints on what we'd like to have. It's how I got my kitty tree, so I can climb almost to the ceiling. Hey! Why the sudden stop? I could have hurt the already-hurt mouse!"

Their human had suddenly stopped the truck in front of a house having a garage sale. She got out, telling her animals that she'd be right back.

"Hello!" the human called. "How much are you asking for that wooden dollhouse?"

"I'm asking $8, but it really isn't finished," a woman in a lawn chair answered. "The other pieces are in the box beneath it. My daughter got it for Christmas last year, and she and her dad started putting it together. But then she went from being 10 and liking dollhouses to acting 16 and following the movie stars. Father and daughter are fighting like two dogs over the same bone, not getting along like they used to, so I'm selling one of the bones of contention—and I'm keeping the money."

"I'd like to buy the house and whatever else goes with it," the human returned. "Hey, does that toaster work?"

"Works fine. Want to try it? I got a four-slice toaster from my kids because this one didn't toast fast enough."

"Good, I'll take both. Good luck with your sale. You've got a perfect day for it."

"It's been going fine," said the woman as she took the $10 bill. "I've made enough money to go to the new day spa in town, and I'm hoping to make enough to make it there twice!"

"Look, guys," their human said, getting back into the truck, "the mouse can live in this dollhouse—just like the mouse on TV! We can adapt it for Whatever-His-Name-Will-Be, and he'll have stairs to run up and down too. I just hope he won't chew the thing to pieces. But, for $8, it's worth a try. Oh, yes, I got a toaster too. Now, we can have toast and jelly while we camp!"

Belle and Jake were certainly impressed with Russell's new accommodations.

"The way our human is caring for your comfort, Russell, you'd never know she was so reluctant to have a mouse for a pet," said Belle. "You are going to live in style!"

They all arrived at the pet-supply store in a happy mood, and their smiles were returned many times over as they made their selections. Belle collected compliments as she rode in the kitty pack. She even helped sell a couple of kitty packs! Now, if she could get paid for being a salescat, Belle thought, she'd buy a kitty fountain so she could have running water all the time, not just when she could catch her human brushing her teeth or washing her hands.

They went to the small-animal department and picked out a watering tube, a dish, food, and other things for

Russell's new house.

Russell peeked out the mesh side of the kitty pack only occasionally. All the people frightened him. "Belle," he explained, "if you're small like me, this is *not* a wonderful place."

"It is a wonderful place, Russell. You're just a bit overwhelmed right now," said Jake.

"If you say so," Russell replied, but he thought he'd stay home the next time.

At the checkout, the cashier greeted them with a smile and a treat. "Thank you for coming in," she said. Then the cashier whispered, "We've sold three kitty packs in the past 20 minutes. Would you like to come in again tomorrow?"

The human laughed. "Sorry, we have only a few more days at the campground, and I haven't visited all the places I wanted to yet."

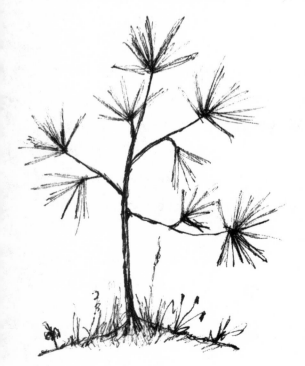

Meeting Alan's Family

During lunch, their human read the instructions for completing the dollhouse.

"This shouldn't be too hard. I'm glad to see the glue bottle is included—I don't have any with my camping gear."

As she worked on the dollhouse, the dog, cat, and mouse spent the time lying in the shade and napping. That is until squeaks and flying leaves announced the return of the chipmunks.

"Hey, Russell, where have you been? We've come by at different times, and none of you were here!" said Alan.

"I've been to the vet, a garage sale, and a pet-supply store," said Russell, even amazing himself.

The chipmunks were suitably impressed, although they had no idea what a vet, a garage sale, or a pet-supply store was, but they sounded scary to them.

"Why did you go to all those places? Did they need an actor?"

"No, I have a hurt paw. See? And I had to get it fixed," Russell

replied. "But the best part is, I think the human is beginning to like me!"

"Russell's going to have a special house to live in," said Jake. "Our human is working on it now. Go over and look at it. She won't hurt you."

Alan and three other chipmunks cautiously climbed onto the picnic table where the human sat. She was concentrating so hard on what she was doing that she didn't realize she had company until one of the youngest chipmunks stepped on the edge of the box and moved it.

"Hi!" said the human, and all the chipmunks ran for cover in the shrubs near the campsite. "Hey, you don't have to run away. I've got some treats for you."

She opened one of the bags of mouse treats she had bought at the pet store and set a small pile on the table.

This time, only Alan was brave enough to climb up, and as he stuffed his cheek pouches full of the treats, he looked at the house that would belong to Russell. Then he scampered off to the brush to share some of the treats with his family, keeping the rest for their dinner.

"Well, Russell, that seems to be a nice place for a mouse like you," said Alan, "but I really don't understand why you want to live above the ground in the open like that. A nice cozy chamber under the ground with family and food is much more to our liking."

"I know," Russell replied. "Your home reminds me of my home with my parents. But this is going to be my own place, and I don't have to hide from the human anymore. She's trying hard to learn my name—though

'Mousey-kins' is not even close."

"That name's from a book," said Belle. "The human read it to Jake and me one Christmas. It's a story about a cat, a mouse, and a cricket. Her guesses could be even more wide of the mark, you know—she does read Shakespeare sometimes."

"She'll learn my name. I just know she will," returned Russell.

"Since you are watching the human making your home," said Alan, "I guess that means you won't be joining us for dinner tonight. We were hoping you could teach our Hazel some of your acting tricks. She's been trying to imitate you since your last visit."

Russell looked over at Hazel, who was trying to hide behind her mother.

"Thank you, Hazel," Russell replied. "That's the nicest thing I've ever heard."

Though uncomfortable with all the attention, Hazel moved away from her mother and offered, "I like your house too, Russell. I like all the sunshine you get to live in."

"I think I will like it too."

"Alan," Hazel's mother said, "it seems our little girl is growing up. She's got a crush on Russell!" she continued, much to Hazel's great embarrassment.

"Come now, Hazel, you know it is the parents' obligation to embarrass their children," teased her father, Alan.

The human wandered over to her pets and was surprised to see them in what looked like a conversation with the chipmunks.

"Though I don't know why I should be surprised anymore," she was heard muttering to herself. "This whole trip has been one amazing thing after another." Then, to the animals, she continued, "Okay, troops, I need to get some serious hiking done. The glue on the dollhouse and furniture will take some time to dry, so we can take a nice long walk in the nature area before I make dinner. Maybe we can see the egret during this vacation. Ah, little mouse, do you want to come?"

Belle looked at Russell, and after he said no, she picked him up, took him into the tent, and tucked him inside the carrier. She then jumped into the kitty pack, ready to go.

"I guess that means the mouse will be staying here," said the human. And, once again, dog, cat, and human were off on another adventure.

"And I've heard people say *we* are never still," said Alan through the door of the tent to Russell in the carrier.

"I don't understand it myself sometimes," Russell replied. "But Jake and Belle seem to want to go with the human anytime they can. I guess I will learn more about people now that I can watch them from my house instead of looking up from the ground."

"How is your paw?" asked Alan.

"It doesn't hurt as much now. And the medicine tastes good—sweet, like a piece of candy I had once."

"Tomorrow, I'll bring the family to see you in your new house," Alan said.

Russell nodded, then snuggled down into the towel in the carrier and went to sleep.

12

A Summer Storm

Jake, Belle, and their human returned after about an hour, and the first thing the human did was to check on the little mouse.

"Yep, still here. I don't understand it, but looks like I'll have to accept it," she said.

The human went over and checked on the dollhouse. The glue was no longer sticky but would need to dry overnight to be as strong as possible for a busy little mouse—one she needed to find a name for.

"Buck?" she tried. "No, too tough. Sweetums? No, too big. Now, I feel like Goldilocks! Argh!!"

The human continued to mutter to herself while she fed the animals and made hot-dog stew for dinner, but none of the names she could think of fit the amazing little mouse.

As all sat by the fire that evening, the breeze started rustling the leaves.

"I thought I had heard thunder in the distance earlier," the human announced. "Well, Jake, I think we should take a quick walk around the park for you to take care of business, so we don't have to do it later in the pouring rain and spend the night in a tent with a wet dog!"

Jake enjoyed his brisk trip around the campground, and the human had time to put out the fire, store the dollhouse in the truck, and get everyone into the tent before the rain started. It was a beautiful storm, with rolling thunder and lightning shows for an hour. At one time, Jake and Belle had been afraid of thunder, but living with their human—who loved storms—had quieted that fear.

Russell whispered to Belle, "Can this thin material really protect us against all of nature?"

"Yes, surprisingly well too," Belle answered. "Our human got this new tent this year. The old one leaked so much that we would spend days trying to get everything dry—including us! Plus, the human is very picky about where she sets up the tent, looking for higher ground and rain runoff patterns in the grass and dirt. We will be safe and dry. Don't worry."

It wasn't until the storm drifted off into the distance that Russell felt it was safe enough to move from his hiding spot. He scurried around, as the others slept, and checked the tent for leaks, then he went to sleep too.

13

Russell Moves In

The next morning, Russell was the last one to wake up, and their human was worried that his paw was giving him trouble again. She checked the cooler to make sure that they had enough ice and that the medicine was still cold. After breakfast, Russell began to perk up and was positively bursting with energy when the human got his house out of the cab of the truck and set it on the picnic table.

She put an old washcloth and some torn paper in the third-level 'bedroom' for him to sleep in and added some things to chew on in the other room—his 'playroom.' On the middle level, she set up the water bottle and a dish of food in his 'kitchen.' And the room downstairs with the front door, she left empty, saying to the animals that she'd make some wood furniture after they got home. Lastly, in the other room on the ground floor, she added a small dish filled with kitty litter.

Belle and Russell were sitting on the table watching their human work, but Jake had to sit on the ground—he was just too big for the table— and watched from where he sat. Then it was time for Russell to move in.

The human got up and went around the table to the other side, opened the door, and gently set Russell in front of the doorway. Even though the whole other side of the dollhouse was open to view, it seemed the best way to move in was through the front door.

Russell crawled through the door and up the stairs. He checked out the food and water in his kitchen. Then he climbed up another set of stairs to the playroom and bedroom, and there, he looked out the window and called out to everyone, "This is the best house ever!"

Their human laughed at the little mouse head poking out of the window and got her camera to take pictures of Russell. She took one of his head sticking out the window, and one of him moving the paper and washcloth to make a comfortable bed, and one going down the stairs, and one eating at his dish, and one of him and Belle touching noses at the front door.

Still holding the camera, the human sat down again to watch Russell from the open side of the doll—now mouse—house.

"I see you found the bedroom, kitchen, and playroom already," said the human. "We'll furnish it with more things and paint it inside and out when we get home. And, little mouse, this room, with the kitty litter, is very important. It is for...um...ah...yes! That is exactly what it is for! You are such a smart mouse!"

Jake moved over to where he could put his front paws on the picnic bench and shoved his nose into the living room of the mouse house. "We always knew you were smart," he said. "But you really won her over now."

"I want to keep my house nice, Jake," Russell replied. "So I can live here, in the open, with you and Belle for the rest of my life. And I'll do anything to show the human I can be trusted."

"You have done that," said Belle. "She's now talking about curtains, wallpaper, and decorating for holidays. You are one lucky little mouse."

The human moved away from the table when she heard the chipmunks in the brush. She watched as they came out into the open and climbed onto the table. Russell met them at the door and invited them in—but only Alan was brave enough to enter. Like any proud owner, Russell showed his chipmunk friend every room—even the attic. The other chipmunks looked in the windows and ran around the outside of the house. And the one room they all thought was the best was the well-stocked kitchen.

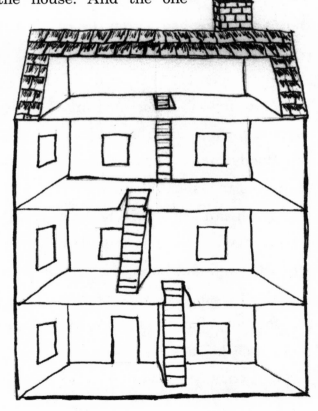

Meeting Someone New

All the animals were surprised to hear a new voice. "You're a rodent, like us, like them—what are you doing in a cage made by a human?" The park's squirrels had gotten the news that strange things were happening in lot 38 and came to see.

"It's not a cage!" exclaimed Hazel, to everyone's surprise. "And Russell is not an ordinary mouse."

"Thought you were the 'shy' one," said the head squirrel, Buddy, sarcastically. "It was made by a human and contains a rodent—it *is* a cage."

"Russell can leave anytime he wants. It is not a cage," replied Hazel. "He has friends and family who can come to visit him in his house. He's special, and you are just jealous."

Buddy the squirrel was stung by the idea that he was jealous of a mouse, especially since it was pointed out to all by the littlest chipmunk in their part of the park.

"Come on, guys," said Buddy. "This is getting bizarre. Let's get out of here before we catch something."

"Hazel, that was really a courageous thing you did for me," said Russell.

"It wasn't courage. It was anger. Those squirrels think they know so much and are no help with all their 'rodents have to stick together' talk. And I really like your house too."

"Thank you," Russell returned. "I was treated with kindness at your home, and I'm glad I can invite you into my new house." And he surprised Hazel with an affectionate nibble on the ear.

Hazel scurried behind her mother, embarrassed again, but happy. The most famous mouse in the whole park liked her!

"Our Hazel's found the courage to speak out—that's something we can thank you for, Russell," said Alan. "She's not going to be the shy one anymore!"

Unnoticed by the animals, the human had been taking photos of the chipmunks visiting Russell in his new house.

"These are wonderful pictures," the human whispered. "There's got to be something I can do with all of them. Hmm, maybe there is…if only I could find him a name."

After Russell invited each of his guests to take a treat home, the chipmunks scampered away.

"If we're going to get any kind of bird-watching in before lunch," the human said, "we'd better be off. Ah, Belle, would you ask the mouse if he wants to go with us? I'd like to go over to the boardwalk on the beach to see if the flock of cedar waxwings are here this year."

"Well, Russell, do you want to join us?" asked Belle. "Seems our human is sure I speak 'mouse' well enough to translate her request."

"Who will watch my house? I don't want those squirrels to get near it!" said Russell.

"Like you could scare them all by yourself, Russell. You're only one little mouse," Jake replied.

"I know," said Russell. "But, if I'm protecting my home, I can be pretty fierce."

"I'm quite sure our human will put your house in the truck again," Belle put in. "She knows how destructive squirrels can be. Remember the flower bulbs last fall, Jake? And the bird feeder in the winter, and the decorated bench she bought for the garden this spring? Not a decoration left on it anymore. And I won't even mention the tomatoes the squirrels have eaten this summer!"

"Then why does she feed them peanuts?" Russell asked. "I saw her, with my own eyes, encourage one of the squirrels at home to take it right from her hand!"

"Because she falls for their con job every time," said Jake. "Sometimes, I can't believe it myself. She says they're cute and won't let me chase them—until they get her tomatoes! That changes her mind for a while."

"Well, if the three of you are finished discussing the world's situation," said their human, "I think we'd better be going. I want to put the mouse house in the truck—will the mouse be going with it?"

"If you put it in the truck, I'd like to join you on your hike," said Russell as he walked over to Belle and sat by her front paw.

"Looks like you want to go with us, little mouse. You are so smart. I wonder, how does Einstein sound for a name? Maybe Albert?"

Russell exchanged looks with Belle and Jake, then turned his back on the human and curled his tail around his body.

"Another 'no' I see," said the human. "Maybe I should get ideas from everyone. I'm having a tough time finding the right name for you."

A Busy Day

Their trip to the beach area was very pleasant. They saw a lot of birds, including the cedar waxwings, and watched the waves stirred up by the previous night's storm crash up on the shore. Even Russell seemed to enjoy the view from the kitty pack. Maybe he could get used to going on walks. He would get to see things that were only stories before.

On the way back to their campsite, they stopped off at the host site to invite Ray and Cheryl to see the mouse house.

"That's something we'd like to see," said Cheryl. "We told our grandson Kevin about your mouse, and he'd like to bring his rat to meet him. What do you think?"

"I wouldn't mind at all," the human replied. "I'd really like to meet his pet rat. I now find myself doing a lot of things that I would have never considered before. If that makes any sense to you," continued the human. "We had quite a party with some chipmunks this morning. I'll show you the pictures I took with my digital camera."

"We'll give our grandson a call and come by this evening," said Ray.

"We like being hosts here in the state park. It gives us a chance to spend time with our grandchildren—otherwise, we're two hours away from them. And they are growing up so fast. Kevin's in high school now!"

"And grandchildren are so much more fun than children!" Cheryl put in.

"That's what my grandma used to say," replied the human. "You can spoil them and then send them home! We'll all look forward to your visit tonight."

When they returned to the campsite, the mouse house was removed from the truck and placed on the table. Then the human set Belle and the kitty pack down too. After her tether was attached, Belle climbed out, and Russell scrambled up and over the edge of the pack and dashed into his house. He went into every room to make sure nothing had changed. After a nibble and a drink in his kitchen, he went up the stairs to his bedroom and buried himself in his bed. He really needed a nap.

Belle and Jake spent the afternoon alternating between sleeping in the sun and resting in the shade. Their human spent the time writing, and later, after she had picked up her book, she would stop reading when an idea popped into her head and add some scribbles to the pages she had written on earlier. The human seemed excited about whatever it was, Belle noticed. Maybe she had some good guesses for Russell's name.

It was later than usual when dinner was finally ready. Chicken and dumplings took a little more time—and made a little more mess—but the results were so good. Russell had a bit of dumpling, while Jake and Belle got both dumplings and chicken. Camping definitely meant more people food for animals.

"We have to do the dishes right away. We're having company tonight. Jake, do you want to wash or dry?" asked their human.

"I'll wash," Jake answered. "You won't know the plates were even used when I'm done with them!" Jake knew their human would do all the work herself, but just in case she was serious, he thought he'd offer.

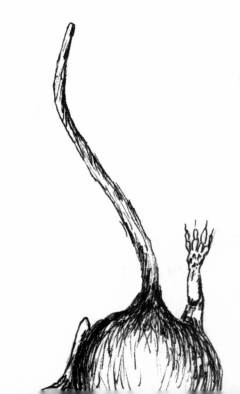

Another New Friend

Just as their human finished setting up the paper, twigs, and branches for the evening's fire, Ray and Cheryl and their teenage grandson Kevin stopped in. Kevin's rat had on a collar and leash and was riding on his shoulder.

"Hi!" said Kevin. "I hear that you have a very special mouse, and he has his very own house. This is Larry. He's my pet rat. I've had him over a year now, and we do a lot of things together—including visiting my grandparents!"

"Pleased to meet you, Kevin—and Larry. This is my dog, Jake, my cat, Belle, and the mouse is in his house. I haven't found a name he likes yet."

"Nice to meet all of you—Larry meet everyone." And Kevin set Larry on the table.

Belle and Jake were suspicious of Larry.

Belle hissed, "Who do you think you are? I know all about rats."

"You know city rats. Me? I'm different. I'm a 'lab' rat—sort of," said Larry.

"What's a lab rat?" asked Russell.

"A rat who bravely spends his or her life helping humans."

"So why did you say you're a lab rat—sort of?"

"Well, because I'm sort of a mistake. My mother was bred to help research one disease, and my father was bred for another, and the two were not supposed to meet. But they did, and the researcher gave the results—me and my four sisters—to a small pet shop owned by her uncle. Kevin came in and picked me out, and we've been a team ever since."

"A team? Is that like a family?" Russell asked.

"In a lot of ways, yes, it is," replied Larry.

Belle still did not trust this fast-talking rat and kept a close watch on him—leash or no leash.

"Would you like to come and see my house?" offered Russell. "It's not painted yet, but it has all the comforts a mouse needs."

Larry looked in the lower rooms and stretched up to see the next floor, showing off how high he could reach. Russell met Larry nose-to-nose at the second level's floor.

"My bedroom and playroom are on the next floor up," said Russell. "And I have an attic too."

"Yes, this is certainly an out-of-the-ordinary kind of home for a mouse," said Larry. "But then maybe you're not an ordinary mouse."

"That's true," said Jake, feeling a little kinder toward Larry. He had sniffed Larry's tail and back while the rat was inspecting Russell's house, and he couldn't smell any of the 'wildness' he found in other rats he had met earlier in his life. "Russell has quite a growing reputation in the park," Jake continued. "He has a squirrel green with envy and a little chipmunk pink with admiration."

"I don't think I'm anything special," said Russell. "Belle rescued me from the cold, and she and Jake have been my family ever since. Their human didn't know I was part of the household until this trip. She seems to be taking it well."

Their human was showing her pictures to Cheryl and Ray and talking with Kevin about the care and feeding of rodents.

"Larry is smart as well as handsome," said Kevin proudly. "He hangs out with me and my friends at my house, travels in the car, visits Grandma and Grandpa, and even helps me with my science project."

"What kind of project?" asked the human.

"We're doing a color-recognition experiment. I'm also including my parent's dog, Skip, and my sister's cat, Butterscotch. Even though dogs aren't supposed to see colors like we do, Skip has been pretty good at figuring things out."

"I've always believed that my animals could see colors," the human said. "Maybe you can experiment with different backgrounds with the colors."

"Yeah, that's a good idea—wow, something else to test for. I'll certainly have enough data to analyze," Kevin replied happily.

Ray whispered, "We're very proud of our grandson. With his interest in science and his wonderful grades in high school, we're hoping to finally have a doctor in the family!"

"Well, Kevin," said the human, "maybe that smart brain of yours can help me out. I've been trying to think of a name for this little mouse. So far, he hasn't liked any of the names I've come up with. I'm looking for suggestions."

Cheryl, Ray, and Kevin declined the honor of naming the newest member of the human's family, and Jake was very happy about that. "Names are what we are," said Jake. "Only someone who knows us should be the one to find our name."

17

The Ice Cream Place

"I have an idea," the human announced. "Why don't we walk over to The Ice Cream Place—my treat? I really appreciate all the help you've given me, and I want to thank you. I must admit, I usually go there most every day when I'm on vacation, but this year, I haven't been there once."

"I wish we could join you," said Cheryl. "But we have plans to go to a dance at the VFW."

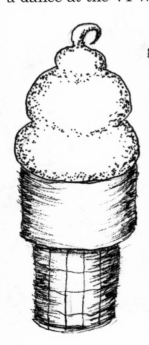

"How about this," suggested Ray. "You and Kevin go get the ice cream, then he can give you advice on raising your very own rodent."

"Great idea!" the human agreed. "Kevin, would you join me for dessert and teach me about rodents?"

"That would be fun, and we'll be able to take all the animals with us."

"Super. Jake and Belle love ice cream," said the human. "But I'm not sure about the mouse."

55

"How does the mouse travel?" Kevin asked. "In your pocket?"

"No, he joins Belle in the kitty pack and looks out through the mesh sides. No one knows he is there, and he gets to see everything."

It was an interesting group walking down the road to get ice cream—Kevin with Larry on his shoulder and the human with Jake on the leash and Belle (and Russell) in the kitty pack. The human ordered a medium ice cream cone with a spoon. That way she would have enough to share with everyone. They sat at one of the tables outside and watched the people play miniature golf next door. For Belle, the human scooped up some ice cream on the spoon and let the cat lick it off. Jake got some of the icy treat and a bit of cone. And Russell and Larry got to split the crispy bottom section of the cone.

While they ate, Kevin gave very entertaining instructions on how to raise a rodent and made everyone laugh—but the humans mistook the animals' laughter as 'getting fussy,' so they started to walk back to the campground.

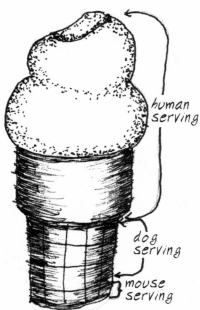

human serving

dog serving

mouse serving

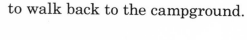

cat serving →

Buddy the Squirrel Returns

"It's hard to believe this is our last full day here," said their human while preparing breakfast the next morning. "We've got to make the most of today."

"It will be a good breakfast for me if you drop a couple of those sausages," said Jake. "I'll even share half of one with Belle."

"I can beg for myself," Belle put in. "And she'll even cut them up for me."

As their human was cooking, the squirrels ran along the branches in the trees overhead. Soon, an acorn came down and bounced off the table—then another and another. And one bounced off Russell's house and landed on the table. By now, everyone was looking up into the trees—and wondering what was going on!

Russell came out of his house and closely examined each acorn that landed on the table. If it wasn't wormy, he moved it next to his house—if it was wormy, he rolled it off the table. When he had a nice pile of acorns, he called up into the trees, "Thank you for the acorns, Buddy. That was a very nice thing to do. I really appreciate them."

From the trees came an angry 'Aaarrrgghhh!'—and the rest of the squirrels all followed Buddy to another part of the park where there weren't any little mice living in dollhouses.

"Russell, they were not trying to be nice," said Hazel, peeking out of the hole by the tree root. "They just wanted to make you scared. Those acorns are too green to eat—they'll make you sick."

"I know, but I wanted to make a point with Buddy. That's why I thanked him for the acorns—his mean plan would fall through when I thanked him for a kindness. Where is the rest of your family, Hazel? I wanted to see everyone today. I'll miss you all when we go home tomorrow."

"You could always stay with us, Russell. I hear there are some mice living over by the rangers' house," said Hazel. "Then we could visit most every day. Mom and Dad will be here in a while. Oh, someone's coming—bye!"

"Wow, breakfast smells good around here," said Kevin as he entered the campsite. "I just wanted to give you my e-mail address, so you can let me know when the mouse has a name."

"Thank you," the human replied. "And I'll give you mine. Then you can tell me how your color-recognition experiment turns out."

"Great!" Kevin continued. "Hi, Jake, how's camping today? And, Belle, how are you? Hey, little mouse, what's piled by your house?"

"We've been under attack by the squirrels," explained the human. "They were bouncing acorns off everything. The mouse would look over the ones that landed on the table and keep the ones he wanted."

While the humans talked, Russell crawled into his kitchen and picked up a peanut, then he brought it out and over to Kevin. "Will you take this to Larry? We leave tomorrow, and I'd like him to have it."

With a puzzled look, Kevin picked up the peanut and asked, "What does he expect me to do with this?"

"I don't know," answered the human. "Maybe you can put it in your pocket, and he'll think you are saving it for later."

"Thanks, little mouse," Kevin said to Russell as he put the peanut in his pocket. "You know, I think I'll give it to Larry."

"It takes humans some time to understand us," Belle explained to Russell. "And sometimes they still never get it right no matter how hard we try."

"Well, I've got to get going," Kevin announced. "Remember to e-mail me when you finally figure out the mouse's name. Bye."

Enjoying the Day Together

"All right, everyone," said the human, "now that the excitement has died down a bit, we'll be able to walk over to the day-use area and down the old railroad trail. I hope to do more bird-watching and get some pictures. We're going to stuff our time full of fun. Little mouse," she continued, "your paw has gotten better fast. Do you want to come with us? I'll bring some lunch and water for all of us. That way we can take time to appreciate what a perfect summer's day this is turning out to be."

Belle, Jake, Russell, and their human did enjoy the day—as friends do when they spend time together. Even the butterflies were happy to have their pictures taken when they were not busy teasing Belle. All shared lunch in one of the observation towers on the preserve and stopped for dessert at The Ice Cream Place on the way back to the campsite.

Their human stopped at the rangers' station to ask about the weather forecast for the evening and was happy to hear rain wasn't expected until the next afternoon. They wouldn't have to pack up wet or make the two-hour trip home with a wet dog smelling up the cab of the truck.

The last campfire had to be perfect because it'd be another year before they would come back. Dinner was another matter, usually consisting of leftovers from the cooler. Jake liked finishing up the bits and pieces not worthy of being lugged home. Belle teased him about being the mobile trash disposal.

Russell left his mouse house and went to visit the chipmunks to tell them he would be leaving the next morning.

The human watched Russell run off and said, "I always thought I'd be glad to see the mouse go back to the wild, but now, I'm afraid he won't return. Maybe I should send Belle after him."

"He'll come back," Belle purred.

"Smokey. I should have asked him if he liked the name Smokey," the human sadly sighed to herself as she started the evening's fire.

Russell was happy to see Alan's whole family waiting for him.

"We had such a nice day," the mouse said. "And I'm sad that we have to leave tomorrow morning. Belle and Jake tell me that we will come back again, after the snow melts and the hot days come again. I think that is a very long time, and I'm afraid you will forget me by then."

"How can we forget you?" Alan the chipmunk replied. "You've become legendary. Stories about you will be told all through the hard, cold winter days."

"And, when I have a family of my own, I will name all my kids Russell—after you!" said Hazel, much to her own embarrassment.

Russell laughed, thinking about the squirrels' reactions when hearing the name 'Russell' being called from every corner of the park. "Why don't all of you join me at my house. We are having everything but pancakes!"

As their human served Jake and Belle their dinners, she smiled when she saw the little mouse return. Then she laughed in surprise. He brought the whole bunch of cute chipmunks back with him.

"Time to get the camera," the human said. "And I'll have to add more bits of cookies and peanuts to his plate."

The animals really put on a show for the human and her camera. She got pictures of Jake nose-to-nose with Alan while they were discussing squirrels, and Belle jumped onto the table next to the mouse house and posed for a photo with Hazel and her sisters. Russell, ever the host,

encouraged his guests to take the leftovers home with them and have 'remembering' meals. Their cheeks stuffed with goodies, the chipmunks left when it started to get dark.

Jake insisted on having a good walk before snoozing by the fire. He had to leave a few pee-mails for the dogs that would be coming to the park after he left. And Belle and Russell discussed the long ride home.

"At least you will be more comfortable riding with us, instead of being packed in a box," said Belle.

"Yes, but it was one of my best performances, pretending to be a stuffed mouse," Russell returned.

"Now, you get to play an adventurous mouse," said Belle. "That's so much better. You get to see more, smell more, and lie in the sun if you choose."

"I will try to have the best adventures," Russell replied.

"Do that, and she may call you Lewis or Clark," laughed Belle.

The evening held one more surprise for the human. As everyone sat in front of the fire, Belle jumped up and lay in the human's lap, and a short time later, Russell climbed up and joined Belle.

"One very unique mouse," the human whispered.

Packing Up

The next morning, when their human awoke, she rolled up her sleeping bag. Belle and Jake knew that this was the beginning of packing to go home. Jake refused to give up his sleeping blanket. Instead, he became limp and heavy.

"Come on, Jake, move it," said their human in exasperation. "You'd think you guys understand that we're leaving this morning."

"We understand a lot more than you think we do," Belle replied. "We look forward to our vacations as much as you do. Don't I always begin to purr when you call me your camping cat?"

In spite of the animals' being uncooperative, their human was able to pack their things and clean out the tent. She made them all breakfast—cinnamon toast! And she remembered to toss some pieces by the chipmunk hole, a last treat for the entertaining creatures.

"Too bad the people across the road left Wednesday. They could have had the fun of watching me take down the tent too."

"They wouldn't have enjoyed it as much. You're too good at the take-down part," Jake grumbled.

So their human put the tent in the back of the truck, then moved the animals into the cab. Jake tried one last time to convince their human to stay by insisting he had to go deliver some pee-mails and needed a walk. When they returned, he had to sniff every corner of their lot while the human did the final 'once over'—to leave the campsite cleaner than when they arrived. Lastly and most reluctantly, Jake consented to being buckled into his traveling harness in the truck. And the ride home began.

With a stop in Otisville for lunch, each began to look forward to getting home. They would talk about this vacation for the rest of the year, and after Christmas, they would begin to plan the next one.

21

The Holiday Letter

"So what does all this writing and stamping and stuffing of envelopes have to do with Christmas?" asked Russell.

"These are Christmas cards," explained Jake. "They are something humans like to get in the mail—they're not bills, advertisements, or catalogs. Christmas cards are pretty and sometimes bring a note or letter from a friend."

"And some of those are more boasting than sharing," Belle added as she jumped onto the desk. "Our human has been writing her own letters to send out—and we're in most of them!"

"Read the best one you can find, Belle," Jake said.

"Ah, that would be the one to Doctor Rhoads," Belle returned. "*Dear Doctor Rhoads,*" she continued, beginning to read the letter, "*yes, the mouse finally has a name!! Jake was helping me wrap the Christmas gifts that had to be sent in the mail. He'd taken a whole roll of wrapping paper and tore it into pieces too small for me to use, and then Belle brought the mouse over to the pile, and she was pretending to hunt for him. The mouse*

would run under the paper and pop up here and there, waiting for Belle to pounce. I was watching them and laughing when I heard the papers rustle again as the mouse scurried away from Belle's paws. Russell!! I called out the name, and the mouse's head popped up. He came running to me and sat looking up at me. It's the perfect name for him, and best of all, he seems to like it.

"*In other news, Jake was in our community theater performance of* Pirates of Penzance. *He got to wear an eye patch and sing with the pirates in the first act and again in the finale. He was a smash hit.*" Belle stopped reading and said, "Yes, but in spite of all Russell's help, you still didn't sing the words right."

"The audience liked it," Jake replied, smiling.

Ignoring the comment, Belle started reading again. "*Belle's nose was a little out of joint when Jake got all that attention, but she's perfected walking on the leash in the neighborhood, and now, we have everyone looking for us when we come down the sidewalk.*" Once again, Belle looked up from the letter and boasted, "Well, at least I got what I wanted—most of those people have adopted kittens and cats, hoping they'll turn out just like me."

"*Lastly, my news,*" Belle continued reading. "*I'm having a book published about Jake, Belle, and the mouse. I wrote most of the story while we were on vacation, and I used the photos I took for illustration ideas. I had my sister edit the book—it's something she does for a living (but she did it for me for free). Then I submitted it to one of the smaller publishers who prefers working with first-time writers—and they liked it! A few changes were made here and there, but it's our story—though everyone thinks I made up the whole thing! Later in the spring, I'll be able to send you your very own autographed (by all of us) copy of* Introducing Russell!

"*You know, I'm pretty lucky. I have a great family—one that includes a cat, a dog, and now, a mouse!*

"*For now, I'll just sign myself as...Their Human.*"

The End

Animals have always held a special place in Debbie's heart. Growing up, she was the neighborhood "go to" person for questions about a hurt critter or a sick pet. And, over the years, she has rescued many animals who were brought to her dead-end street and left to fend for themselves. All this firsthand experience has given Debbie a one-of-a-kind chance to observe the habits, behaviors, and attitudes of our four-legged friends—and it's given her some very unique stories about the special relationships that can develop between animal and animal… and, even more so, animal and human.

Also holding a very important spot in Debbie's large heart is her love for children—attested to by her two grown boys (who continue the Walter tradition of sharing their homes with beloved pets). With her fondness for education in one hand and her years of working in an elementary school's library in the other, it was only natural that a children's novella would flow from Debbie's talented and creative soul.

Introducing Russell, which Debbie also illustrated, reflects her cheerful and caring spirit and brings her love of nature and animals to children of all ages.

Moose Run™
Productions

A publisher of books that offer readers a wholesome and enjoyable respite.

Moose Run Productions publishes books of various genres that are wholesome, decent, and uplifting.

If you would like a **free** copy of our catalog, please visit our Web site at moose-run.com or complete and send this form to:

Moose Run Productions • P.O. Box 46281 • Mount Clemens, Michigan 48046-6281

Name _____

Address _____

City, State, Zip _____

E-Mail (optional) _____